All rights reserved. No part of this work may be reproduced or stored in an information retrieval system (other than for the purposes of review) without the express permission of the publisher in writing.
© Copyright 2012 Jim Green

1

As the murky 1950s steam train chugged and spluttered its way towards Platform 2 of Preston Station the assembled passengers reacted like automatons, picking up their hand luggage and taking two steps forward en masse in preparation for boarding; forty-seven minutes later than scheduled.

Among those present was a disparate couple. The swarthy figure of Ginger Harrison with his unruly crop of carrot red hair was a full head shorter than his companion Sticky Albright, a rangy beanpole with a pronounced slouch.

'That's the best part of an hour's drinking in Blackpool we've just lost,' said Ginger testily as he scanned the passing carriages for a vacant compartment, 'and with no corridor, there's no bar on this clapped out people carrier'

'There's an empty,' observed Sticky who in a rush to claim the cubicle dropped his weekend valise spewing its contents onto the platform; shirts, socks, ties, underwear, and a large bright pink floppy object.

'What the chuff is that?' enquired Ginger.

'It's Bartholomew, my teddy bear'

'Bloody Norah, why did you bring that with you?'

'I can't get to sleep without him'

'So I'm expected to share a bed with a frigging teddy; not bloody likely'

'It's okay; I keep Bartholomew under my pillow at night'

'Well get the bugger stored away or we'll be put down as a couple of whoofters – and don't be showing him off to the tarts we take home from the dancing tonight'

Sticky was crestfallen. 'But Ginger you promised you'd behave this weekend'

'And I will, no overdoing the ale, no punch ups and no arrests – but I didn't make any promises about crumpet. I'll be having my share of whatever comes along'

An elderly man of the cloth was about to open the door of their preferred compartment when Ginger intervened. 'Sorry, your reverence, but this one's taken, reserved like'

The clergyman looked around for evidence to that effect but could find none.

'There is no reserved notice on the windows,' he gently countered.

'It probably blew away down the tunnel back there; notorious it is for things blowing away what with the wind whistling through at the double'

'You can produce tickets of reservation then?' enquired the cleric.

'Oh aye, we can that,' replied Ginger as he pushed Sticky aboard, followed suit, and slammed the door tightly shut leaving the bewildered ecclesiastic in limbo on the platform.

*

The exterior of the Balmoral boarding house, situated in a side street off the South Shore, had recently been redecorated in a particularly dazzling shade of yellow and from an upstairs hallway window the landlady Mrs Moakler was looking down on the refurbishment with marked satisfaction. She had a crown of curlers adorning her newly permed henna hair and a cigarette wedged between her vermillion lips as she turned and called out to someone downstairs, 'They've made a nice job of it'

'What was that Mrs Moakler?' replied a squeaky female voice over the strident hum of a vacuum cleaner.

'I said, oh never mind, I'm coming down'

The landlady started to descend but stopped at the mirror in the sub landing to view her appearance. With hands on hips she turned her torso to the left, looked over her shoulder and commented silently on the reflected profile, 'Not bad for fifty-four; bum and tits still firm; some mileage left yet in the old boiler'

'I said,' she continued on reaching the ground floor, 'they've made a nice job of painting the outside. I like yellow, it's fresh and friendly, don't you think?'

'Oh aye, it is and all Mrs,' agreed the squeaky voice which belonged to Elsie who acted as general factotum around the establishment; cook, housemaid, cleaner, and all manner of ancillary duties. She pondered before adding above the steady whine of the cleaner, 'Cheerful like is yellow'

'Switch that damn thing off while I'm talking to you Elsie,' and when her request was granted Mrs Moakler carried on, 'and don't forget you still have the beds to see to upstairs, not just for the weekend guests but all fourteen rooms; we have a full card with Monday's intake and I want them all ready today; not tomorrow or the following morning. Is that understood?'

'Yes Mrs Moakler,' confirmed Elsie, 'I'll make start as soon as I'm done down here and I'll be finished come lunchtime'

'Good, oh I hate Saturdays when the place is all but empty, I much prefer Mondays because you know where you are on a Monday with the whole week planned out ahead. Now, who have we got in over the weekend?'

'Just the old couple we've had before who go to bed while seven o'clock of an evening and two young men from Irlam; at least that's what Doris has got written down in the book, "Two young men from Irlam" '

'Two young men from Irlam,' scorned Mrs Moakler.

'She'd better smarten her ideas up that Doris or she'll be back in the dole queue. It could be Jack the Ripper and friend for all we know'

'Jack who missus?'

'Oh, it doesn't matter, get cleared up downstairs as soon as you can'

*

Ginger's rotund and recumbent shape was dozing fitfully across the entire seating area of one side of the compartment when his slumbers were interrupted by Sticky's reminiscing. 'Those were great times Ginger when we were appearing in clubs and theatres as Brylcreem and Brasso; remember?'

Ginger cocked an eye open. 'I could hardly have forgotten; that was only four years ago; just after we were demobbed from the RAF'

'Pity it came to an end; the money was good and I enjoyed all that travelling around the country'

'Yeah well, nothing lasts forever, does it; double-acts, especially comedy, fell out of favour with the cash paying patrons'

'I remember our last performance'

'So do I, the toilet seat that pillock chucked on the stage almost brained me; it missed my head by no more than an inch. If I'd found out who did it I'd have flushed his head down the nearest loo pan'

'Wish we could have carried on,' lamented Sticky dolefully, 'I miss the stage, the companionship, the money; the chorus girls'

Ginger sat bolt upright and glared at his friend. 'Stop your mithering, we came out of it okay with enough brass to start a business didn't we – and we got to keep the name, *Brylcreem and Brasso, Scaffolders to the Nobility* is who we are now'

'Bad mistake that was Ginger, some folk call up and ask for Mr Brylcreem and if he's not in, Mr Brasso; other folk reckon our prices must be rip off because we cater for toffs – which we don't'

'You have no sense of reality Sticky,' chided Ginger, 'You got to have flair in business nowadays if you want to make your mark. Brylcreem and Brasso is our stock in trade; it's goodwill, it's what makes us stand out from the competition, the crappy scaffolders who don't know their arse from their elbow - and what's more – there are other folk who remember Brylcreem and Brasso as a stage act and put jobs our way because of it. Now give over moaning and let me get some kip'

'Do you think Mrs Moakler will remember us?' asked Sticky undeterred.

'She'll remember you okay; you got your leg over there last time we stayed with her'

'That's only because she felt sorry for me and took me into her bed when you shoved me out into the hall to sleep'

'And she gave you a brand new suit; her old man's wasn't it?'

'Aye, I wonder if he still goes out singing hymns in the street with that big red-haired piece'

'You can ask her about that when you see her – now shut up'

*

In another compartment in the same train and heading for a night out in Blackpool was flamboyant Hazel Rigby and her mousy friend Chrissie Bulstrode; Hazel filing her nails and Chrissie engrossed in a copy of *True Romances*.

The formidable Miss Rigby was a big busted peroxide blonde of statuesque proportions whose lemon top and short black skirt clung so closely to her body they could have been sprayed on; Chrissie in comparison was plain and prissy and wore a drab dark brown blouse over unfashionable fawn culottes.

'We'll have to leave the dancing early to catch the last bus home,' bemoaned Chrissie, 'and all because this sodding train is running late and there's not another one back to Irlam after nine o'clock'

'Who said anything about catching the last bus? We might get fortunate and hook up with a couple of guys with transport'

'With our luck it's more likely than not to be a lorry'

'Better than hoofing it'

*

'Ginger'

'What is it now?'

'You're not really thinking about bringing tarts back to Mrs Moakler's tonight, are you?'

'If we find any and they're willing, of course I am you dozy prick'

'You know what's she's like; she'll toss us out on the street'

'No, she'll toss me out on the street; she'll toss you off in her bed'

2

Elsie stood at the foot of the stairs and called up, 'Mrs Moakler, the two young men from Irlam have just arrived'

Down floated the reply from upstairs, 'Tell them I'll be down directly'

With the curlers banished and hair now in a stylish bouffant Mrs Moakler checked in the bathroom vanity mirror for potential blemishes, reapplied lipstick, powder and eyebrow pencil, gently teased her hair ends, dabbed scent liberally behind the ears, patted her bottom as if to substantiate its firmness, and to round off matters, farted thunderously to make herself comfortable before greeting the new arrivals.

Although the black cocktail dress she wore was a size too small it served nevertheless to show off her shapely curves to advantage as she descended the stairs to reception, waggling her ample rear en route.

Without looking at her guests she repaired behind the desk and opened the reservations register.

'Two nights then, bed and breakfast, is that correct?'

'That's right Mrs Moakler,' validated Sticky.

'I recognise the voice,' and raising her eyes continued, 'Cedric, I am so pleased to see you again'

'Cedric, did you say Cedric?' gasped Ginger unbelievingly.

'It's my given name,' said Sticky blushing.

'Well, bugger me and dress me up in the cat's pyjamas, I never knew that and I've been in your company for going on six years'

'Are you still with the Rosicrucians?' enquired Mrs Moakler pointedly of Ginger. 'I remember you saying you were a follower'

'Ah,' he suffered a fleeting moment or two of memory loss before his powers of recall came to the rescue. 'Yes missus, whenever I can, at the services they hold up the tent hall of a Sunday morning'

'You do your readings from the Almanac; I thought that a bit strange'

'Eh?'

'Last time you were here you told me that Rosicrucians always use the Almanac as their book of prayer'

'Oh aye, that's right; Old Moore's Almanac for preference when we can lay our hands on one'. Ginger suspected that much more of this inane questioning would engulf him in even deeper waters. 'Well, best get signed in then'

'That will be six pounds each,' replied Mrs Moakler in a business like tone.

'Bit steep isn't it?' protested Ginger. 'Last time you only charged us three pounds for the weekend'

'That was then - this is now'

Having signed the register and forked out in advance the two young men from Irlam ascended the stairs, found their room and began to unpack. As Ginger picked up his toiletries in preparation for an early wash and shave he remarked, 'By the left Sticky that was a close call. The old bat don't forget nothing; I wonder what else she remembers'

'She'll remember the night we brought back the drunken GI'

'Oh aye, she wouldn't forget that; it was the same night she had her wicked way with you'

There was a brisk knock, the door open fractionally, and a hennaed head appeared. 'Cedric love,' it said, 'could I have a private word with you, in my room, you know where it is' and then vanished.

'Here we go,' observed Ginger, 'she wants you as her plaything for tonight'

'I don't know as I do,' replied Sticky doubtfully, 'she'll get all amorous when I go into her room, opening my shirt buttons and running her hands up and down my back'

'There's plenty who would pay for what you'll be getting for free'

'I don't know…'

'Go on lad, have some fun; you're on holiday'

'But what about you, what will you do on your own?'

'I'll be alright; I'll have a few ales at Yates Wine Lodge and go up the dancing'

'Promise me you won't bring any tarts back'

'I was only having you on about that Sticky lad. What chance would I have picking up tarts and talking them into coming back here? Look at me, I'm a fat bastard'

'Well, if you're sure you'll be okay…'

'Of course I will, enjoy yourself. Oh, I've just thought, ask her for a front door key. I don't want to be coming back here early; I want to get a few ales down me, relax; unwind'

Some minutes later Sticky arrived back looking distinctly uncomfortable.

'Did she ask you?' enquired Ginger.

'Aye'

'Did you get the key?'

'Well, she was going to give it me and then when I said I'd think about it, spending the night with her I mean, she pulled a right face, went all huffy like, and said the front door closes at ten-thirty prompt and don't get opened again until next morning'

'You bloody great long twat, how the hell am I going to bring tarts back to the room now?'

'But Ginger, you promised…'

*

After disembarking at Blackpool Central Station, Hazel and Chrissie made for the Super Eats cafeteria situated behind the Tower where they were dining on a strict budget.

'Three and sixpence for a rotten salad,' complained Chrissie, 'it's a disgrace; there's not enough lettuce on this plate to feed a baby rabbit'

'You should have had roast beef and chips like me,' responded Hazel as she munched her way through a forkful of particularly tough silverside.

'And the tomatoes are off'

'Well, they say salad is healthy food; good for you'

'It's not doing much for me'

'Did you notice the thickset ginger haired lad and his lanky mate get off the train at Blackpool South?' asked Hazel.

'Aye, I did, why?'

'They run a scaffolding business at premises just down the road from where I live'

'Irlam lads, do you think then?'

'Not as I know for sure but it's where they run their business like and they've got funny names, Brylcreem and Brasso, it says so on the rickety old van they drive; wonder which is which?'

'Maybe they're foreigners'

'Happen they are'

'They were carrying luggage so they must be here on holiday; we'll maybe come across them later'

'Look the other way if you do'

'Why?'

'They're nowt but labourers; we can do better for ourselves tonight than those two'

*

Back at the boarding house Ginger was putting the finishing touches to his attire for the evening; open-neck short sleeve shirt in a vibrant shade of green, red cavalry twill slacks and brown suede shoes with brothel creeper soles.

'You're not still mad at me are you?' enquired Sticky timidly.

'Nay lad, if you don't fancy a night of passion with the landlady, that's okay by me. We'll go down the town together and have ourselves a ball'

'Where will we go to start?'

'Yates Wine Lodge, forced to be, it's traditional on the first night; then on to the Winter Gardens for a touch of the light fantastic and some crumpet'

'We'll not have much time there; she shuts up shop at ten-thirty remember'

'Half past ten o'clock be bolloxed; we'll stay out as late as we like'

'But the missus will have locked us out'

'So we'll have to find another way in, won't we?'

'What about something to eat, I haven't had a bite since breakfast and I'm starving hungry now'

'We grab some sandwiches at the pub'

3

As always on Saturday nights Yates Wine Lodge was packed to the gunnels but using his rock solid girth as a battering ram Ginger soon cleared a passageway through the massed crowds of pleasure seekers; a path in which Sticky meekly followed. When he reached the bar rail Ginger yelled, 'Two meat pies, two cheese rolls, two pints of best bitter and two shorts!'

A nearby patron took exception to his opportunism and protested, 'I'm before you in the queue to be served; I've been stood here for the last ten minutes'

Short on remorse, Ginger replied brusquely, 'That's your hard bun mate; you should learn to shout louder,' and turning to Sticky instructed, 'you go find us a table lad'

'But there's none spare; they're all taken'

'Then you stay here and pay the barman while I go negotiate with some punters who already have seats. I'll be over at that table,' at which he pointed to two middle-aged men supping from pint pots, 'and when I give you the nod, start shaking'

'What?'

'You heard me, just shake like fuck when I give you the nod, and keep your eyes on me while I'm talking to them'

Ginger approached the unsuspecting twosome and opened the conversation with, 'See that bloke at the bar, the tall skinny one with the dopey look'

They turned to observe Sticky and one of them commented suspiciously, 'What about him?'

'The poor sod suffers from St Bodolf's falling down disease; in a minute he'll start shaking and then he'll be flat on his arse on the floor'

'Are you some kind of nutter?' asked the second member of the twosome. 'I've never heard of any saint by the name of Bodolf'

Ginger nodded to Sticky whose frame started to tremble from head to toe.

'Just watch, in a few seconds he'll fall down'

'You'd best have our seats then,' said the first member,' we wouldn't want the silly bugger hurting himself' at which they picked up their pint pots and departed with Ginger calling after them, 'Bless you lads, you'll get your reward in a better place'

Ginger indicated to Sticky to join him and he arrived carrying their food and beer. 'I'll have to back for the shorts,' he said, and added, 'what was all that about?'

'I'll explain later'

*

From another table near an exit Hazel had been monitoring the interface and shouted to Chrissie over the din that enshrouded them, 'The fat lad from Irlam got two old guys to give up their seats for him and his mate. I wonder what he said to them'

*

'This is the life Sticky, beats the hell out of scaffolding; maybe we should sell up and move to Blackpool. We could get a concession at one of the piers and who knows, maybe break back into show business'

'You still haven't told me how you got those old duffers to give up their seats – and why the hell did you get me shaking like that; I felt like a prat'

'Well it worked didn't it, so why all the fuss?' He paused for a moment then continued, 'Hold up, what's occurring over there, two young damsels in distress and if I'm not mistaken, an opportunity to grab some spare crumpet'

Sticky looked over in the direction to which Ginger indicated where one girl was being pawed by a bearded lout while the other, a blonde, appeared to be fending off unwanted advances from his mate.

'Now Ginger, remember what we agreed, no trouble this weekend; no punch ups, no coppers feeling our collars, no nights in the clink'

'Relax lad,' replied Ginger as he got on his feet and made to depart, 'just you sit there, finish off your meat pie, sup your ale. I'll just go check that those girls are okay and while I'm away, don't go falling flat on your arse'

'You what?'

As Ginger approached the scene of would-be disturbance the blonde girl at the table slapped one of the louts roughly across the face at which he burst out laughing.

'Are you ladies in some difficulty here?' enquired Ginger evenly.

'Fuck off fatso and mind your own business,' snarled the beard.

Ignoring the outburst Ginger repeated his question.

'No, we're alright, we can handle this,' replied the blonde.

'Well I can't,' contradicted her friend, 'this creep won't stop mauling me'

'We can handle it I said,' snapped her companion.

'No lady should ever have to,' gallantly countered Ginger who then turned to address the louts sotto voce, 'I have a three-way proposition for you two. You can leave peacefully, or I can take both of you outside, or I can do you individually. So what's it to be; one at a time or as a group? Makes no odds to me lads'

The louts stood up and the beard said, 'It doesn't need both of us to sort you out, you tub of lard'

'Fine,' said Ginger, 'let's step outside friendly like and I'll give you a sample to stick on the end of your knife' Sticky arrived on the scene beseeching Ginger to avoid confrontation.

Ginger whispered in his ear, 'There's no call for commotion lad; I'll just take this prick round the back and stave his nuts in, quiet like'

Less than thirty seconds later he returned alone, flexed his enormous biceps, and suggested to the second lout, 'You might just want to check on your mate; he slipped on a piece of banana peel on the way out and busted his nose'

'You don't sound like you come from foreign parts,' observed Hazel as the remaining lout hurried away.

'Eh?'

'Well, I've never come across a Brylcreem or Brasso before…'

'How do you know we're Brylcreem and Brasso?'

'I've seen it on your van in Irlam'

'That's not our real names,' explained Ginger, grinning broadly, 'he's Sticky Albright and I'm Ginger Harrison'

Chrissie had been absorbing every second of the proceedings in wide-eyed awe while the glint in Hazel's eyes betrayed reluctant approval of the manner in which Ginger had coolly and skilfully controlled a potentially explosive situation.

*

In the dining room at the boarding house Elsie's eyes were on the other hand welling up with tears as she confided in the elderly couple prior to their customary early retiral for the evening.

'She's in a right black mood Mrs Moakler is tonight; as nice as ninepence all day she's been to me and now she's turned really nasty, finding fault with everything. I'm right fed up I am. One more complaint and I'll tell her where to shove her rotten job'

'Don't take on so dear,' comforted the wife, 'maybe she's had some bad news, maybe something someone else did is upsetting her and she's just taking it out on you'

'Things will be back to normal tomorrow morning, you'll see,' added the husband.

'Elsie!' screeched a voice from upstairs.

'Coming Mrs Moakler,' squeaked Elsie, 'coming straightaway'

*

'So how did you come by the name of Sticky?' enquired Chrissie earnestly. The wine was flowing freely now with the banter keeping equal pace between the extrovert Ginger and Hazel who alternated on bursts of frenetic laughter as they teased one another with sensual barbs. Sticky and Chrissie conversely shared an uneasy silence broken only by occasional questions.

'I used to be a plasterer's apprentice,' Sticky enlightened her thoughtfully.

'Aye, until he got his fingers caught in the till,' goaded Ginger at which Hazel giggled uncontrollably.

'Cut it out, you're giving them the wrong impression about me; I never did no till dipping. When you're apprenticed to a plasterer you can't help getting sticky lumps on your overalls'

There were more giggles when Ginger riposted, 'And that wasn't the only thing that got sticky – especially when the big lass in reception pranced around the workshop wearing a see-through blouse and waggling her arse'

'Fuck you Ginger Harrison,' flared Sticky.

'Now, now, manners please, watch your language, ladies present'

Hazel smoothed the way when she intervened with, 'Have you two always been scaffolders?'

'Nay lass, we used to be in show business, comedy double act; that's where we got the name Brylcreem and Brasso'

'Get off, you two were never on the stage'

'Oh aye, we were that alright,' confirmed Sticky with conviction, 'topped the bill three times at the Bradford Men's Working Club, appeared in pantomime and did summer seasons all over the place'

'Here Sticky,' enthused Ginger, 'remember the time we shared a dressing room with The Great Farto when we were just starting out and still doing national service'

'Who did you say?' asked Chrissie innocently.

'What a performer, The Great Farto, never seen anything like him since'

Hazel demanded to know, 'What kind of bloody act was that?' and added under her breath, 'as if I didn't know already...'

'He appeared onstage dressed in a purple leotard with a blow torch as a prop – '

'And farted non-stop for five minutes,' interrupted Hazel, 'then stuck the torch against his arse and whoosh, flames and smoke all over'

'How do you know that?' asked Ginger in astonishment.

'My dad used to take me to the Rochdale Empire and Farto was on the bill every other week until he set the frigging place on fire one Friday night'

'Did you get burned?' enquired Chrissie concernedly.

'No, but The Great Farto did; the theatre manager took the blow torch to Farto's arse – when he wasn't farting –

he was hospitalised for three months and never worked again - at least not with a farting act'

'Well I'll be buggered,' summarised Ginger.

'Aye, he used to do a lot a of farting,' mused Sticky, 'and not just on the stage; our dressing room needed fumigating twice a week'

Hazel looked Ginger straight in the eyes and said, 'You must be worth a few bob with all that topping the bill like'

'Oh aye lass, rolling in it,' and turning to Sticky continued, 'the tide's gone out, go and get some more ale in, there's a good lad'

As Sticky made to rise, Chrissie contributed, 'I'll go with him'

'Good girl, you pay and let him carry the drinks back'

'So, what plans do you and your mate have for tonight?' asked Hazel when they'd gone.

'Thought we'd go up the Winter Gardens; care to join us? We could have some more ale, some dancing, some smooching and who knows what else afterwards'

'We reckoned on the Tower Ballroom'

'You don't want to be going there,' scorned Ginger, 'that place is always full of drunks and layabouts of a Saturday night'

'It's too late now anyway; we'll have to shove off soon if we want to get home tonight'

'Don't be rushing off so early, the night is still young, there's plenty more drinking time left – anyway we can put you up for the night'

'Oh aye, own a hotel do you as well as a scaffolding business?'

'No but our landlady has a few rooms going spare'

'We couldn't afford it'

'There's no need; Sticky and me will take care of it'

'No thanks, you'll want your oats in lieu of payment'

Ginger adopted a pained expression and replied, 'Now I ask you, is that nice; an act of friendship and you suspect the worst.' Crossing his fingers he added, 'Maybe you'd best just leave now if that's what you think of us'

'All right, you're on – but no funny business - or I'll knee you in the groin'

Sticky and Chrissie returned laden with beverages and as she passed the drinks around Chrissie nudged Hazel, 'We'll have to leave after this round; it's going on ten o'clock and the last bus leaves at half-past'

'No need,' replied Hazel briskly, 'the lads are putting us up for the night – and before you ask – we'll have our own room'

'We can't,' shrieked Chrissie, 'my mam will go spare if I don't come back home tonight'

'No she won't, she'll be best pleased. Whichever old soak she picks up at the pub won't have to bunged in the coal shed until you come in and shoved out the back door at half past five in the morning'

With noticeable satisfaction Sticky threw a well-aimed spanner in the works, 'Makes no difference either way. The boarding house front door closes at the same time your last bus leaves'

Hazel glowered at Ginger and shouted, 'you bloody great far arse; what are we going to do now!'

'We'll have to sleep in a shelter along the promenade,' wailed Chrissie.

'No you won't, relax everyone, I'll get us all in,' assured Ginger, 'you'll soon be sleeping soundly in a warm bed, and waking up to a slap-up breakfast'

4

There was a handwritten note pinned to the front door of the Balmoral boarding house addressed to the two young men from Irlam.

It read 'Don't knock on this door or ring the bell. If you do I will call the police'. It was signed by Mrs Moakler.

'What now mastermind?' said Sticky smirking.

'No problem lad,' replied Ginger, 'I'll just shin up the drainpipe, climb through into our bedroom, and back down here to open the front door. Be ready with your shoes off; we don't want floorboards creaking and waking up the old bat'

'You'll never get the window open; I put it on the latch'

'And I took it back off again before we left'

'You crafty bugger,' said Hazel, 'you planned all this in advance'

'Well, you do, don't you?'

With the skill of a seasoned scaffolder Ginger scaled the drainpipe, vanished through the bedroom window, and was back downstairs within sixty seconds with a finger poised on his lips and motioning the party to follow him.

'This is a bit of all right,' said Hazel on entering the bedroom, 'is this ours?'

'All yours my dear, all yours,' replied Ginger beaming broadly.

Sticky tried to intervene but was staunched in his tracks by the other young man from Irlam, 'Feel free if you want a scrub down before hitting the hay girls; I'll use the bathroom after you'

'What do mean you'll use the bathroom after us,' snapped Hazel, 'use your own'

'But it's communal; we'll be sharing like, the bathroom and the bed'

'You can fuck off out of it right now; I meant what I said back in the pub, come anywhere near this bed and I'll knee you in the groin so hard your ardour will take a permanent nosedive – I mean it'

'I'm off out it myself anyway,' said Sticky picking up his belongings and heading for the door, 'I'll wake up Mrs Moakler; she'll take me into her room'

'Good idea Sticky lad, oh, and tell her I met my sisters down the promenade, they missed the last bus and we've given them our bed for the night; you could say I'm sleeping out in the corridor'

'She'll come up and check'

'Okay, I'm sleeping in the bath then'

'She won't believe that either'

'She'll swallow it if you tell her at the right time'

'What time?'

'Just after you've potted her'

'I give up, I'm off'

'Here lad,' pulling back a pillow and removing the pink teddy bear which he tossed in Sticky's direction Ginger cautioned, 'don't be leaving Bartholomew behind on his own now; he might get lonesome'

'Bastard,' muttered Sticky departing rapidly.

The girls looked at each other in disbelief and Hazel gasped, 'He's got a teddy bear, a bloody pink teddy; he's fucking queer him, queer as a four-pound note'

'No he's not lass, as the landlady will testify in the morning if you ask her'

'Do you have a teddy under your pillow as well?' enquired Chrissie nervously.

'Nay, lass, would I, I ask you now, would I?' he responded in a bruised tone, 'I keep mine out of sight, under lock and key back home - and now girls, you wouldn't really have me sleeping out in the corridor, would you?

'Yes we bloody well would, you're a nutter you are' responded Hazel firmly, 'just collect your gubbins and piss off out of it'

'He could sleep in the bath,' suggested Chrissie tentatively, 'it won't be so cold; he could have a blanket and a pillow after we've finished in there'

'Well, okay then,' mellowed Hazel reluctantly, 'make yourself scarce in the corridor for the next ten minutes while we get ready for bed'

Ginger tossed and turned in the cramped bath for what seemed like hours and just as he was settling into a sleep of sorts the door opened, the light was switched on, and there stood Hazel with her right hand on the door jamb, posing provocatively in the nude.

'Come on then you great lump, you'd best join Chrissie and me in bed; we don't want you catching your death of cold, do we…'

'Oh, thanks lass' replied Ginger gratefully.

*

Next morning Sticky trudged upstairs and gently knocked on the door at which a voice bade him enter. Ginger was sitting upright in bed with a smile a mile wide and the girls either side of him.

'Getting to know each other a bit better then,' observed Sticky snidely.

'Aye well, the girls reckoned I might be cold in the bath like and persuaded me to join them for a bit of a warm up'

'Did you show the landlady your teddy?' enquired Hazel mischievously.

Sticky ignored the barb, shrugged his shoulders, and said, 'she says you and Chrissie can have breakfast on the house'

'That's very civil of her,' reckoned Ginger.

5

Elsie looked much more cheerful as she served the elderly couple their breakfast, 'She's back to normal is Mrs Moakler; even made me a cup of tea while I was scrambling Binky's eggs'

'Who's Binky?' asked the husband looking around the dining room.

'Must be one of the four at that table in the corner,' suggested the wife, 'there's no one else around'

'No, no, missus,' corrected Elsie, 'Binky is her toy poodle, she dresses him up with pink and blue ribbons and he's even got his own room'

'Fancy,' said the husband dubiously.

Ginger gestured to Elsie and with pad and pencil to the ready she scurried across the room, 'Ready to order now?'

'Aye lass, these three will have the full English but no tomatoes for Hazel, she reckons they give her the hump''

'Get off you cheeky devil,' riposted Hazel.

'And I'll have pig's trotters with plenty of mustard, oh, and a curried pickle on the side'

Elsie's jaw moved up and down nervously as she stammered, 'p-pig's t-t-trotters of a morning?'

'Aye'

'But we don't serve pig's trotters for breakfast. Mrs Moakler wouldn't allow that; she'd say it was common like'

Ginger sighed and replied, 'Very disappointing that is Elsie. All right, just give me the full English as well – and I'll have the lass's tomatoes'

As Elsie was departing Mrs Moakler made an entrance, cracked a smile at the elderly couple and approached the foursome.

'Well, well, well, these two young ladies are the surprise guests I take it'

'Aye missus,' corroborated Ginger solemnly, 'my little sisters, Hazel and Chrissie, always been close we have, my little treasures as you might say; they light up my days'

'And your nights,' muttered Sticky under his breath.

Ginger proceeded to explain the circumstances of the girls' arrival at the boarding house, 'I saw them standing at a bus stop last night, up from Irlam they were for the day and they'd missed the last omni. Freezing cold my little lasses were; I couldn't have them walking the streets so I brought them back here'

'Slept in the bathroom yourself I hear'

'Forced to, wouldn't have it any other way; you've got to take care of your own'

'Very gallant I'm sure'

Mrs Moakler's gaze scanned Ginger, Hazel and Chrissie in turn, 'I can't say as I spot any family resemblance,' she remarked.

'No, you wouldn't,' said Ginger serenely, 'we're from different fathers you see; our mam was a right little goer in her day'

'At it like a rabbit,' confirmed Hazel cogently, 'and she wasn't fussy who she did it with'

Feeling obliged to make a contribution Chrissie added, 'Yes, I heard tell she had lots of friends'

'Evidently,' concluded the bemused landlady.

As she made to walk away, Ginger asked, 'How is Mr Moakler these days; still singing hymns in the street with that red-haired hussy is he?'

'Don't ever mention that pair to me again,' she bristled, 'living over the brush, living in sin; no better than animals. They should be locked away'

When she had departed Ginger reviewed his little band of playmates and enquired, 'Now what shall we do today?'

'Do, we'll not be doing anything, we have to go home now; my mam'll be going spare' replied Chrissie.

'No she won't,' contradicted Hazel, 'when she discovers you're not back yet she'll have another session with the old bugger she picked up last night'

'Now Hazel,' protested Chrissie, 'that's not fair, my mam is not like that'

'Not much'

'You could send her a postcard,' suggested Ginger.

'She wouldn't get that while Wednesday,' Hazel pointed out not unreasonably.

'Well, a telegram then'

'I wouldn't know what to say in it,' said Chrissie, softening somewhat.

'Sticky will look after that for you – and he'll pay for it; he's generous that way'

'Now hold up a minute,' Sticky intervened.

'You will, you're generous almost to a fault, you are. Remember the time in the RAF when we were doing befriending and you gave old Obediah Outhwaite all them shilling coins to fill up his gas meter?'

'No I didn't, you stole them; you broke into the cash box in a telephone box'

'That's as maybe, but you were the one who sorted out the shillings from all that filthy copper. I could never have done that, but you did, and all to help out an old man in distress'

'Yeah, well...'

'That's settled then; a telegram to Chrissie's mam it is'

'I've never been up the Tower,' exclaimed Chrissie, 'could we do that today?'

'Never been up the Tower, what never?'

'No Ginger, I always meant to but never got around to it'

'Well, we'll soon put that to rights, you can't come to Blackpool and not visit the Tower; it's sacrilege that is. But first though we'll have a stroll along the prom and see what's occurring; maybe have our photos taken as a memento like'

'I could ask Mrs Moakler for packed lunches,' volunteered Sticky.

'Good idea lad, you see to that, and we'll be on our merry way'

6

In the security department offices at Blackpool Tower the superintendent of operations Wilberforce Jordan was addressing his accolades, 'I want you all to be particularly vigilant today because as you well know we get a right lot of nut cases in here over the weekend'

'Someone crapped in the lifts last night,' volunteered one of his crew.

'Yes, yes, yes,' snapped Jordan, 'there's no call for detail on particular incidents; just keep your eyes peeled and your hand on your wallet. Now Hoskins, I want you to concentrate exclusively on the observation deck; we don't want no sky diving from drunks or larking about from tearaways. Any sign of trouble and you report it to me on your walkie-talkie straightaway. Got that?'

'Sir'

'Right then you lot; be off about your business, and remember, Blackpool welcomes its visitors with an open heart but we do not allow the buggers to wreck our Tower, now do we?'

'No sir,' chorused the duly primed workforce.

*

Having negotiated the Golden Mile on foot and sampled most of the attractions along the way, the two young men from Irlam and their newly acquired girlfriends arrived at the Tower laden with candy floss, balloons, paper hats and streamers. They purchased entrance tickets and headed off towards the lifts that would take them to the observation deck.
Tagging them with the label of potential troublemakers, the security officer assigned to the elevators spoke earnestly into his walkie-talkie.

'By the left, that was quick,' said Ginger appreciatively as he and his companions emerged from the lift, 'considering the height we travelled'

The dozen or so other sightseers milling around the deck disappeared inside in ones and twos as the icy breeze strengthened its bite, leaving the foursome on their own leaning against the rail surveying the panoramic vista.

'We're 380 feet up,' announced Sticky, 'and on a clear day you can see as far as North Wales, the Lake District, the Trough of Bowland and as the sun sets on a clear evening, the Isle Of man is visible across the Irish Sea'

'Bloody hell, a walking travelogue,' observed Hazel.

'I read that in a brochure and memorised it'

'That man keeps looking over at us,' said Chrissie anxiously.

The other three looked over to where she indicated and Ginger assured her, 'Don't heed him, he's just a security wallah, but if it bothers you I'll tell him to shove off'

'No, no, it's okay'

'380 feet you reckon Sticky,' continued Ginger, 'that would make it about 400 feet to the crow's nest at the top'

'So?'

'So I reckon I could climb it'

'All the way up from here past two platforms and the steel girders in between, no chance, not even a skilled mountaineer would think of scaling that'

'But maybe a skilled scaffolder would'

'I'll bet *you* wouldn't'

'How much, how much will you bet?'

Sticky pondered for a moment before suggesting, 'A fiver?'

'Listen to him, a fiver, a measly fiver,' scoffed Ginger, 'make it fifty quid and I'll do it right now'

By now Hazel and Chrissie were becoming intrigued over the outcome of the challenge and Sticky sensed their mounting interest. He would look chicken if he backed out and on the plus side it seemed to him like an easy way to pick up fifty pounds; he reckoned Ginger would have second thoughts before reaching the second of the daunting platforms leading to the crow's nest.

'All right, you're on, fifty quid it is'

'That security man is still watching us,' remarked Chrissie.

'I'll get rid of him,' volunteered Hazel.

'You mean, like lead him on, oh I don't know about that, lass,' replied Ginger doubtfully.

'Don't worry, I'll get rid of him in a flash, just watch,' and with that she approached the watcher. 'Got a light have for my fag?' she asked him.

He took a box of matches from his pocket but after a few attempts at ignition announced, 'The wind's too strong; we'll have to go inside'

'Okay, you lead the way, I'll follow,' said Hazel smiling broadly at him.

'What's she playing at now?' asked Sticky.

'You'll see, if I know her, she'll lose him fast,' answered Chrissie.

Indoors the security officer Hoskins cupped his hands together and held a lit match close to Hazel's face; all the better to run his gaze up and down her statuesque body.

'You're a big boy; are you big all over?' she flirted.

'Well, I've not had any complaints,' he preened.

'Oh, I'd love an ice cream cone, but I can't face going all the way back down'

'I'll get one for you,' he offered.

When Hazel returned she declared, 'I've sent him to get me ice cream and I promised him a lick when he gets back - if you know what I mean'

'But he'll be down and up in no time, you saw yourself how fast the lifts are,' cautioned Sticky.

'Not where I've sent him he won't; I told him I can only eat ice cream from the parlour up beside the Winter Gardens. There's always a big queue there so he won't be back for ages'

'Now girls,' proclaimed Ginger with mock severity, 'inside with you at the double while I strip off'

'You're not thinking about any monkey business out here are you?' asked Hazel, 'you're off your head if you think Chrissie and me are joining in'

'No monkey business out here my love,' he assured her, 'only on the girders. I'm going to hang my under drawers on the flagpole on top of the crow's nest'

Shrieking with laughter the girls rushed off indoors while Sticky shook his head and pleaded with Ginger, 'No, think about it, don't attempt that, you might fall off'. He paused for a second before adding, 'not the drawers with the skull and crossbones all over, not them surely?'

'Aye, that's the buggers'

'You can't drape them over the Union Jack'

'No, no, of course not lad, that would be disrespectful; I'll take the flag down first and replace it with my knickers'

'You're fucking crazy, you'll get six months in the nick; that's – that's interfering with the Queen's standard that is'

'I'll be 400 feet up; nobody will see me'

'I wouldn't be too sure about that; there's always people gazing up at the Tower from street level '

'Not right now they're not; not with the gusty gale blowing up down there'

With the skull and crossbones pennant secured firmly between his teeth Ginger eased his backside over the rail, grasped the steel girders immediately above with both hands, and disappeared onto the first of the platforms leading to the crow's nest.

A few minutes later the girls arrived back and Hazel asked a worried looking Sticky, 'He's gone up then has he?'

'Aye, he has, the mad bastard'

'Well, it's only a bit of fun'

No longer concerned over losing a bet and more exercised about foregoing his freedom, Sticky retorted, 'Bit of fun, bit of fucking fun; we'll all end up in clink over this'

'Bloody marvellous this,' shouted a faint voice from above, 'you can see even better from up here'

'Is that Ginger?' asked Chrissie unnecessarily.

'No, it's your mam,' rasped Hazel, 'she wants to know which bus we're catching'

Sticky leaned out over the parapet and called up, 'Come back down Ginger; that security guy will be snooping around again any minute now'

Prophetic words as it transpired because Hoskins appeared clutching two ice cream cones. He handed one to Hazel saying, 'There was a queue but I managed to shove up to the front being as how I'm in official uniform'

'Oh, that was handy,' replied Hazel without conviction.

'Would you like to come for a stroll? I could show around the security offices,' and winking added, 'it'll be quiet there at this hour of day; no one about like'

Just then Ginger materialised over the rail and this time clutching the Union Jack between his teeth. Hoskins dropped his ice cream cone on the deck and scarpered back indoors. An alarm bell went off followed by the piercing sound of a siren. As the young men from Irlam and their girlfriends rushed to the nearest lift, the doors opened and out came six burly guards, two of who grappled with Ginger while the others escorted Sticky, Hazel and Chrissie downstairs.

7

'Wheel them in then,' barked Superintendent Jordan to one of his crew and in trooped Ginger, Sticky, Hazel and Chrissie. 'Well, well, well, 'exclaimed Jordan with pronounced surprise, 'the fat bastard and the long streak of cat's piss; I knew I'd come across you two scallywags again one day, I just knew it'

'How does he know you and Ginger?' whispered Hazel in Sticky's ear.

'He used to be our sergeant in the RAF; he'll have us put away for life,' groaned Sticky.

'Old Bandy Jordan, now there's a blast from the past, a sight for sore eyes, but not for mine', greeted Ginger cheerfully. 'How do you like it here then sarge; I mean what with having no parade ground to strut around in like?'

'Don't call me Bandy and none of your lip lad; you're in serious trouble, all of you. I'm calling in the police; your high jinks up the Tower will get you but one thing, the high jump. Climbing up to the crow's nest and removing the royal standard, they'll lock you up and throw the key away; the royal standard and you an ex-serviceman'

'Well,' mitigated Ginger in his defence, 'I did leave my underpants in its place'

'You did what?' exploded Jordan, 'you'll wind up in the bloody Tower of London, you will, you – you sodding saboteur!'

'Okay then, have me charged if you must, but let the other three go; they had nothing to do with any of it'

'Like hell they didn't; you're all in it, bloody anarchists'

Another security officer burst into the room proclaiming, 'There's someone outside to see you Mr Jordan; he says it's very important'

'Tell him to piss off,' shouted Jordan, 'can't you see I'm busy'

'He's a reporter from the Blackpool Gazette'

'Reporter, newspapers, we don't want any of that – okay - tell him I'll be out in a minute. Hoskins, watch this lot while I'm gone, and if any of them as much as sneezes, call out loud'

'Sir'

Jordan marched smartly out of his office into the anteroom. 'What can I do for you?' he asked the visitor.

'Not so much what you can do for me as I can do for you'

'What do you mean? Explain yourself'

'The unusual behaviour at the top of the tower'

'Unusual behaviour, there's been no unusual behaviour, none whatsoever'

The reporter handed Jordan a newly processed black and white photograph and said, 'This was taken by a staff photographer with a telescopic lens at the time of the incident and processed immediately; it's fuzzy but not too fuzzy to identify a young man clutching the flagpole with one hand and the Union Jack in the other. I understand you have the young man in your office and are no doubt interrogating him right now

Jordan grimaced and responded, 'A minor matter; it's being attended to'

'Minor matter, don't try to kid me, you could lose your job over this'

'I'm just about to call the police; they'll handle it'

'Well, it's up to you of course, but if you do that you run the risk of having yourself and your department investigated'

'How do you mean?'

'Investigated for proficiency in maintaining security within the Tower precincts'

'Hmm well, yes…'

'I have a proposition that will get you out of your difficulty unscathed'

'What proposition?' asked Jordan suspiciously.

'Forget about calling in the police; let me take over the matter. What I have in mind is a human interest story that will be snapped up by every national newspaper in the country'

'National newspapers, you must think I'm as daft as the fat bastard who climbed up the flagpole. I'd rather take my chances with a police investigation'

'You'll be sorry. If you agree to a re-enactment of the incident I'll have you rescuing the young man from the crow's nest; you'll be a hero – and I'll give you one hundred pounds for your participation'

'Re-enactment, did you say? I'm not risking my bloody neck at the top of the Tower for a stunt'

'There's no danger involved; you'll be in a safety harness and winched down from a helicopter. I will arrange for police authorisation'

'You're off you nut; the chief constable will never agree to that'

'He will when I show him this,' at which he handed Jordan another picture. 'He wouldn't want that published in the nationals instead the shots I'm planning to take'

The picture portrayed the chief constable not in uniform but attired in a red wig, full length ball gown, with an evening bag in one hand and a white rose in the other.

Jordan studied the reproduction for a moment and responded, 'That don't make him a transvestite; you could have had the picture done up like'

'What, and all of these too, done up as you describe?' The reporter handed Jordan a batch of prints displaying the senior police officer in a variety of provocative transvestite poses.

The bewildered security superintendent thumbed through the pictures awkwardly and declared, 'It would have to done after hours, at night'

'That's exactly what I think'

'The fat bastard and the other three would have to agree – and keep their mouths shut afterwards'

'Let me talk to them, in your office'

'Okay, follow me'

8

'What's in it for me then?' asked Ginger when the Blackpool Gazette reporter finished outlining the details of the proposed re-enactment.

'Fifty pounds and your name in all the papers'

'Call it a hundred quid and you have a deal'

'Okay, one hundred pounds it is; you'll be the star of the show, so what's another fifty here or there. And now that's settled, we need a beauty for the beast, like in King Kong'

'King who?' enquired Hazel.

'Kong, a popular film, before you were born I should think. King Kong climbed to the top of the Empire State Building in New York to escape the clutches of authority and in search of his beauty, Fay Wray – and it's funny you should be the one to ask that question because you're the very one I want for the beast's beauty'

'I wish you'd stop calling me a beast,' complained Ginger tersely.

'Figure of speech my boy; just to illustrate the ploy'

'I'm not climbing up the bloody Tower,' asserted Hazel with equal brusqueness.

'But that is, pardon the pun, the beauty of it; you won't have to, either of you. We have a helicopter standing by to winch you and Ginger down into the crow's nest and up again after we've taken a few press photographs. Oh, and the security superintendent will accompany you in the copter'

'What the hell do we need him for?' demanded Ginger indignantly.

'We'll have him on camera descending on a winch to rescue you and Hazel from the crow's nest'

'Bloody Norah'

'I'm still not doing it,' said Hazel firmly.

'Think again young lady before you turn down a golden opportunity to become famous; your picture will feature on the front page of every national newspaper in the land, you'll be inundated with offers of work; photo shoots, modelling – '

'Modelling?' interrupted Hazel excitedly, 'you mean like in magazines and that?'

'Precisely, you'll be the queen of the catwalk'

'Go on Hazel, give it a go,' urged Ginger.

'Okay, I'll do it'

'I'm glad it's not me,' piped up Chrissie, 'my mam wouldn't like me getting my photo took in a crow's nest'

'She'll like it even less when she finds out it's me that was picked' responded a smirking Hazel.

'How about me, how come I'm not involved?' Sticky protested.

'Well, you could be if you wish, holding the cameraman's tripod on the platform immediately under the crow's nest – we could winch both of you down in a separate run'

'How much would I get paid for that?'

'Union rates, somewhere between a fiver and a tenner I should think'

'Bloody hell; Ginger's getting a hundred'

'Come, come, now lad,' soothed Ginger, 'you're an extra; you can't expect a star salary for labouring'

'Piss off

*

Some hours later the re-enactment took place without a hitch and was all done and dusted within thirty minutes. The reporter thanked his cast and crew for their sterling efforts and advised them he had to rush off to another assignment before getting down to work on the feature and its syndication to the nationals.

'My God,' screamed Chrissie, 'we've missed the last bus again!'

'Don't fuss lass,' said Ginger, 'come back with us to the boarding house; we'll have a bite of supper and the landlady will put you up for the night again, proper like this time'

'No she won't,' disagreed Sticky, 'she won't believe that sisters stuff a second time'

'You are so wrong young man, she'll believe anything tonight, 'countered the reporter, 'she's my next assignment and when she learns she is to be in the newspapers too, she'll let you all stay a month if you like'

9

When the little band of mischief makers returned to the Balmoral boarding house they were met at the front door by an ecstatic Mrs Moakler who embraced them all individually. She recounted the details of her visitation from The Blackpool Gazette and concluded with, 'If I'd known he was coming tonight and bringing along a photographer, I'd have had my hair done again. Oh dear, I hope I don't look a sight in the papers tomorrow'

'Never in a million years missus,' Ginger vigorously reassured her, 'you're a fine looking figure of a woman. Sticky, haven't I always said that about Mrs Moakler, haven't I always reckoned she's the most glamorous landlady in Blackpool, haven't I now?'

'Oh aye, happen you have,' mumbled Sticky, 'when I wasn't around to hear'

'That nice reporter chap told me you'd all be coming back here tonight so I've had Elsie lay on a spread for you; I knew you'd be hungry'

'Oh aye, we are that,' agreed the mischief makers in unison.

'Elsie has a treat for you Ginger; she's prepared pig's trotters with mustard; she reckons that's your favourite'

'Oh aye, lovely, thanks missus'

'And girls, you'll have your own rooms tonight; I've made up the best two in the house and they're both en suite'

'En what Mrs Moakler?' asked a mystified Hazel.

'It means you'll have your own separate bathrooms'

Ginger frowned, scratched his head, and protested, 'There's no need to go to all that trouble missus; my sisters can have my bed again – '

'What do you mean; your bed?' intervened Sticky belligerently. 'I'm supposed to sleep there too you know'

'And I'll kip in the bathroom,' came back Ginger robustly, ignoring the outburst.

'Nonsense, nonsense I couldn't allow your sisters being cooped up like that again; it's not seemly, they'll have their own rooms and that's that,' declared the landlady, putting an abrupt end to the discussion.

'Does en thingy have a shower?' asked Chrissie.

'Oh yes dear, and it comes with a variety of flow speeds'

'That'll be nice for you,' muttered Ginger. 'You can shower in strict tempo; flow, flow, quick-quick, flow'

Elsie's repast was consumed in next to no time and Ginger had three helpings of pig's trotters after which the weary party trooped off to their respective bedrooms.

Sticky lay sulking on one side of the bed clutching Bartholomew and Ginger on the other bemoaning his misfortune, 'Bloody fair isn't it, me stuck in here and the girls in separate rooms; she shouldn't have stuck her nose in like that, the old bat'

'What about me, she didn't offer to take me into her bed again tonight'

Ginger propped himself up on an elbow and enquired, 'Did you want her to take you in again? You weren't all that keen last night'

'Aye, I did,' sighed Sticky, 'you get used to it'

'Well, get up and ask her then'

'I think I will'

'And I'll knock on Hazel's door and see if she'll take me in'

Still in their pyjamas the two young men from Irlam tiptoed down the passageway on their separate missions and while Sticky met with instant success, Ginger hit a stumbling block.

'Go on lass, let me in, it's bloody freezing out here,' he pleaded.

'Shove off,' rebuffed Hazel, blocking the doorway, 'you've run me ragged today and I want a good night's kip – undisturbed – on my own'

'But I'm all alone in that room; Sticky's gone off to the landlady's'

'That's your hard luck pal – and don't be thinking about knocking up Chrissie and dragging her back for a threesome – that's not on tonight'

'Okay, I'll ask Chrissie if I can kip up with her,' said Ginger, trying his hand at divide and rule.

'No you bloody don't; if you sleep with anyone, you sleep with me,' and realising how she had completely compromised herself, relented, 'Oh, all right then, come in here you great fat arsed Romeo'

10

Ginger arrived back at the Brylcreem and Brasso scaffolding yard around noon on Monday with a bundle of newspapers tucked under his right arm. He unlocked the door of the mini-office, entered, clicked on the kettle switch, and minutes later Sticky made an appearance. 'You're just in time for tea lad,' said Ginger.

'Have you managed to read all the morning papers yet?' asked Sticky enthusiastically. 'That reporter guy was right; you're in every bloody one of them and on the front page in most'

'I have that, read them all, I have. "*Beauty and the Beast Scale Blackpool Tower; Rescued by Security Superintendent*" says the Daily Mail. Trust old Bandy Jordan to muscle his way into the act'

'I reckon he was just getting his own back for the time you got him pissed, stripped him, and threw his clobber into that stinking canal stream'

'Oh aye,' mused Ginger, 'I'd forgotten about that; he had to walk back to camp bollock naked and every time he walked into the sergeants' mess after that they used to whistle Colonel Bogey, remember? *Bollocks and the same to you*...and what was the other one we used to sing, oh yeah,

> *Stand by your beds*
> *Here comes the air vice-marshal*
> *He's got lots of rings*
> *But he's only got one arsehole*

'Those were the days; I still miss being in the RAF you know' said Sticky sighing.

'As much as show business, do you reckon?'

'Aye, oh, have you talked to the girls since we got back?'

'I spoke to Hazel; she's over the moon at having her mug splashed all over the papers; right made up she is. She and Chrissie are coming up to my flat tonight. How about joining us for a bit of a do?'

'No thanks, I know what kind of a 'do' that will be. Anyhow I've got something to think about myself'

'What's that then?'

'Mrs Moakler stuck a note in my pocket as we were leaving this morning; she wants me to come and live with her at the boarding house. What do you think to that Ginger?'

'Best not I reckon, spring and autumn, it won't last; you'll end up out in the street like her old man - singing hymns with Elsie'

'Happen you're right; I'll give it a miss'

'So you'll come up to the flat then?'

'Aye, might as well, there's not much on telly tonight'

'There never is'

'What time do you want me up?'

'Around eight o'clock I should think - and bring a case of light ales'

Blackpool Ballroom Blitz
Comedic Retrospective from the national service years

'Right lads; it's pay-up time for the Blackpool weekend and I need three quid from each of you. Strictly cash, no IOUs'

Chalky White, in his capacity as organiser and treasurer for the billet outing, had entered Hut 29 carrying a clipboard and fingering the pencil lodged behind his right ear.

'How do you make that out then?' enquired Ginger, 'how come three quid?'

'There's the train fares and an overnight stay at the digs to be accounted for,' explained Chalky exercising due diligence. 'That comes to the best part of three notes each - with a little left over for emergencies'

'What emergencies?' asked Sticky in complete innocence.

'Shut up, you big girl's blouse,' reprimanded Ginger. 'How many rooms are you allowing for Chalky?'

'Three. With six of us travelling, that'll be two people per room'

'We don't need three rooms,' Ginger disagreed vehemently. 'You're throwing away good ale money. We can all bunk up together in the same room like we do here'

'What, six in a bed?'

'You can get four in a double,' asserted Ginger.

'Four?'

'Yeah, two at the top, two at the bottom'

'Jist like back hame,' protested Jock Burns. 'Stuff me'

'Only as a last resort,' qualified Scrounger.

'Count me out of that deal mate.' Spiffy shook his head. 'I ain't having no geyser's smelly feet stuck up my hooter'

'Then you and Chalky can bring your sleeping bags and kip on the floor,' reasoned Ginger.

Sticky, who was meanwhile counting on his fingers, observed, 'That leaves some bugger with nowhere to sleep'

'No it doesn't. We'll fix you up in the bath up with some cushions and a rug'

'Eh?'

'Well,' reflected Chalky cautiously. 'There's some merit in what you say Ginger. Doing it your way will certainly hike up the ale kitty'

'I'll go along with that,' seconded Spiffy.

After some persuasion, Jock Burns, Scrounger Harris and Barry Emerson also agreed to the revised accommodation arrangements.

'That's that then,' said Ginger grinning broadly. 'You'll thank me when there's still money left for a few jars on the way back'

On Saturday morning the party assembled at Padgate station to board the train for Warrington, then on to Preston where they would change to an excursion special bound for Blackpool Central. They carried haversacks, wore casual civvies and had their spear-point collar shirts open at the neck. All except Sticky who was wearing a luminous mustard poplin suit with matching shirt and tie. He was carrying a battered old suitcase.

'That's a wide-awake piece of schmutter, mate,' observed Spiffy.

'Me Uncle Harry give it me. He got it from a Yank when he got torpedoed in the North Sea during the war'

'Your Uncle Harry?'

'No, the Yank'

'You're having a laugh, aren't you?'

'Never mind all that bollox,' broke in Ginger. 'Here comes our train'

Once aboard, Chalky immediately set about his duties as the official outing organiser. He opened up his haversack and withdrew a handful of brochures and leaflets, which he passed around the party. 'These will give you an idea of the amenities and places of interest in the Blackpool area. I thought we'd start with a visit to Stanley Park where we could take a boat out on the pond'

'Pond, whit dae we want a pond fur when we've got the sea?' complained Jock. 'Ah don't see the sense o' that. Anyway, we'd huv tae tak a bus an' that's mair expense'

'Ah, but you see,' countered Chalky enthusiastically, 'After Stanley Park I thought we'd visit the maritime museum nearby-'

'Bloody Nora, Chalky,' interrupted Ginger. 'What do you think you're organising, a girl guides outing?'

'Oh well,' Chalky replied huffily, folding his arms and scowling, 'if that's the way of it, you'd best take over'

'Aye, I will. We'll check in at the digs first, take a stroll down the front, have a dip in the sea, go back and have us teas, get freshened up, call in at Yates' Wine Lodge for a few ales - and then on to the dancing'

'Winter Gardens or Tower Ballroom?' enquired Barry.

'Tower, forced to be'

'Hold up,' interjected Scrounger, 'we don't have no cossies for a dip in the sea'

'Didn't you pack your drill shorts then?' asked Ginger.

'You can't wear drill shorts to bathe in the sea'

'I chuffing can'

'I reckon we should go t'Pleasure Beach,' proposed Sticky.

'The Pleasure Beach, in that suit, they'll stick you in a sideshow, mate'

'Mair likely use him fur target practice at the rifle range,' opined Jock.

'What's the talent like at the Tower?'

'No' bad, but no' as good as the Albert'

'The Albert Hall?'

'Naw, ya mug, the Albert Ballroom in Bath Street'

'What's he on about?'

'Brawest lassies in Glesca go there on Seterday nights,' Jock reminisced fondly.

'Fancy that'

*

Gladys Moakler, landlady of number ten Balmoral Gardens on the South Shore reviewed the new arrivals with unconcealed distaste.

'No alcohol in the room, no smoking, no gambling, no bringing in your own food, no cooking, no shenanigans, no sneaking in members of the opposite sex; is that understood'

'Aye, missus, you're all right there,' confirmed Ginger. 'Would it be okay though if we had us a prayer meeting tonight? We usually do of a Saturday evening'

'As long as you're not Baptists; I'll not have no Baptists in this house'

'How about Rosicrucians?'

'Aye, well, happen.' She eyed Ginger curiously. 'But no Baptists; they give me the hump they do'

'Why is that missus?' asked Scrounger.

'One o't them, big red hair hussy she was, made off with my husband a few months back and turned him into a bible thumping street preacher'

'Leave you a bit short-handed, did it?' suggested Ginger. 'I'll say. He did the shopping, cooking, serving, washing, ironing and bed making'

Spiffy whispered in Barry's ear, 'Bet the old duffer was glad of the conversion. Talk about the Road to Damascus...'

'Front door closes ten o'clock sharp every night- including weekends,' concluded Gladys fiercely.

*

Five open-necked spear-points and one highly luminous poplin suit promenaded along the front debating where to go first.

'I vote the quick flicks,' advanced Scrounger.

'You dirty bugger'

'We could have us photos took,' suggested Sticky, espying some yards ahead a busy street photographer who had a queue of punters forming up

'Good idea. How much are you charging, squire?' shouted Ginger.

'Four bob a go'

'You're opening you're mouth a bit wide,' remonstrated Scrounger.

'How about a discount for national servicemen?' proposed Chalky.

The photographer pulled away from his current assignment, looked them over, relented, and replied as he was resuming his duties, 'Well, two bob apiece for you lads, seeing as how you're doing your bit - but you'll have to wait until I'm through with this lot'

'Sounds reasonable'

'Are we having our photos taken then?'

'You'll be the ones who gets took if you give him two bob each,' warned Spiffy.

'How do you mean?' asked Ginger.

'He's a con artist, ain't got no film in his camera'

'How do you know that?'

'I've seen him on the prom at Margate. He and his mates dodge from resort to resort down the south coast. Makes it difficult for the rozzers to catch up with them'

'What's he doing in Blackpool then?' said Barry.

'He gets on an early morning train in the smoke, travels up here, rooks the day trippers Saturday and Sunday, then vamooses back down south wiv a stash of cash'

'You still haven't explained how you know his camera's empty,' persisted Barry

'Look, it works like this. He clicks away like a good 'un, takes the money, gives the marks a dodgy address to pick up their snaps on Monday - but there ain't no snaps, no film, no address - and he's back down the smoke when they go looking for their prints'

'I just gave him eight bob to have me grandchildren's pictures taken,' contributed an elderly lady who had been eavesdropping on the conversation.

'Did you now mother?' replied Ginger. 'Well, let's have a gander inside his camera. Here mush, give me your magic lantern'

'You what?' exclaimed the photographer, taken aback.

'You heard'

'Piss off. I'll have the law on you'

'No you won't.' Spiffy moved in, eyeballing the happy snapper. 'You've been working the front up and down all day to avoid them'

'Hand the box ower,' growled Jock, 'or ah'll throw you and it in the sea'

'Gerroff'

Ginger snatched the apparatus and opened it. 'You're right Spiffy, no film, as empty as the vicar's collection box. Right, give the lady her money back - plus another two bob so her nippers can have some candy rock as they got no photos'

'Here comes a copper,' observed Spiffy.

'All right, all right, here's ten bob for the old dear. Fine thing when a honest man can't make a living,' complained the photographer, scampering off up a side street.

*

'Hello, come for a sitting, have you?'

It was Stan Withinshawe accompanied by Bunny Hare. They had just spotted the party entering Tussauds wax museum.

'Yeah,' riposted Ginger, 'Scrounger's up for melting down next week. Thought we'd have a look around first'

'Here, we're going clubbing tonight,' said Bunny enthusiastically. 'Would you like to come with us?'

'You'd be perfectly welcome, I'm sure,' added Stan.

'No thanks, we're off up the Tower'

'Ah well, you'll get great views tonight, what with the illuminations'

'They don't need the illuminations,' Stan disagreed. 'That mustard suit will shine like a beacon for miles around'

'Not that tower, the Tower ballroom,' advised Ginger.

'Oh, fancy'

'I'll come clubbing with you,' volunteered Chalky.

*

Yates' Wine Lodge had the usual Saturday night crowd in comprising hawkers, dockers, rockers, navvies, comic singers and dancers. The party found it difficult to make themselves heard above the din and when Ginger was almost through his fourteenth pint, he announced loudly, 'Time gentlemen please,' and swallowing the remains in a single slurp, he thumped the tankard down hard on the counter. 'It's off to the Tower and on with the crumpet'

'Why are we having crumpet now,' enquired a mystified Sticky. 'We've just had us teas'

'No, you dozy beggar,' explained Scrounger, 'he means the talent up the dancing'

*

Three hours had passed without incident at the Tower Ballroom when Ginger turned to speak to Barry in the upstairs spectators' gallery. He had to shout to be heard above the Joe Loss Orchestra as they belted out their version of 'Bewitched, Bothered and Bewildered'.

'Grand night, grand night, good ale, good dancing, good lasses, what more could we ask for?'

'Certainly not what I'm witnessing downstairs,' replied Barry, pointing to a disturbance on the floor.

Ginger looked down. 'Trust some idle josser to ruin everything. Best go sort it out'

Jock Burns had also witnessed the fracas. He'd been standing quietly one his own at the edge of the dance area watching Scrounger displaying his expertise at the slow foxtrot and engaging in animated conversation with a young lady when they were rudely interrupted.

A mountainous GI in dress uniform had pushed Scrounger aside roughly and whisked off his partner in a bear hug. She was pummeling him with her fists in protest at his unwanted advances.

Jock shoved his way through the mass of dancers to the middle of the floor and addressed the Yank.

'Get yir jukes up. It's a square go'

'Go take a walk, buster'

'Ah've hud a walk'

Three other American soldiers made to rush to the assistance of their comrade when Ginger appeared on the scene and with outstretched arms halted their progress.

'You heard the man. It's a square go. No butting in - Marquis of Queensberry rules'

However, as a precaution and to ensure that they fully understood the terms of his dictate, he head butted each of them in turn.

'Hadn't we better give Jock a hand?' said Barry.

'Naw, he'll be okay. He's sturdier than a red brick wall'

Back in the centre of the floor, the Yank released his grip on the distressed young lady and moved in on Jock. He towered over his adversary, advising, 'you don't know what you're taking on here buddy. I'm the va-va-va-va-vroom-boy'

'Oh aye, is'at right Jimmy? Well, here's a Maryhill kiss tae stick on the end o' it,' at which Jock too executed a perfect head butt, knocking the gargantuan Yank in a heap to the floor.

Several burly bouncers arrived belatedly to escort the combatants forcefully from the ballroom.

'Are you okay mate?'

Ginger was endeavoring to help the Yank to his feet where he lay crumpled on the pavement.

'Ouch, no, leave me. I've hurt my foot.' As an afterthought he added, 'And I've missed the last bus back to Burtonwood'

'He can come back wi' us tae the digs,' growled Jock.

'He'll have nowhere to sleep,' argued Sticky.

'Aye, he will. He can have the bath; you can kip in the corridor outside'

'Eh?'

*

The revellers staggered all the way from the Tower down the Golden Mile to the South Shore, Balmoral Gardens and a locked front door. Supporting the lame Yank between them were a bedraggled Ginger and Jock.

'The old scroat has shut us out,' said Spiffy, hammering on the door.

Immediately above them a light was switched on, a window opened, and a head full of curlers emerged. 'I told you ten o'clock. You'll not get in here tonight' yelled Gladys Moakler.

'But we've brought back a wounded American soldier from the front,' protested Ginger equally loudly.

'It's okay but, missus,' added Sticky, ''he's not a member of the opposite sex'

'You what?'

'Wounded American soldier from the front'

'What front?'

'Blackpool front'

'Right, I'm throwing down a key. Catch'

*

Jock had gone out early to accompany the Yank to the nearest bus stop; the others were at table when Sticky strolled into the breakfast room wearing a stylishly cut navy blue serge suit.

'Now that's what I call a tin flute,' remarked Spiffy admiringly. 'How did you come by it?'

'Mrs Moakler give me it, belonged to her old man'

'Where's the monstrosity you was wearing yesterday?' asked Ginger.

'She wrapped it up with brown paper an' string and sent it to Mr Moakler wi' a note inside telling him to wear it when 'he goes out preaching in street'

'Was it cold outside in the corridor last night?' enquired Scrounger.

'Dunno'

'How d'you mean you don't know?'

'Ah weren't in corridor. Ah slept in the missus' bed'

'Where did she sleep then?'

'With me'

*

Jock arrived back with some disturbing news.

'Chalky's up fur sentencin' at the Sunday Court they huv fur weekend trippers that ur out of order'

'What's he done?'

'Got himself arrested at a club Bunny and Stan took him tae'

'Did they get nobbled too?'

'Naw, some pal let them oot a side door'

'Oh, one of them funny clubs'

'Best get down to the court then,' said Ginger.

They arrived at the court towards the end of the proceedings to witness Chalky standing dejectedly in the dock, the object of concerted stern glares from the magistrates on the bench.

The chairman was a short, round little man with flowing locks of stringy white hair. He spoke in a rasping voice.

'We don't hold wi' lewd, late-night drinkin' clubs in Blac'pool where men dress up as women and vice versa, gives the town a bad name. An' we don't hold wi' day trippers what frequents them neither. But seein' as how you're a first offender, I'll go lenient on you like. Fifteen shillin's fine an' bound over for twelve months'

*

'Well, that's it lads, no ale on the way back,' groaned Ginger. 'We'll have to pay his fine'

Why?'

'He's got no brass. I know that for a fact'

'How come?'

'Because there's only fifteen bob left in us kitty I tapped him for yesterday morning'

'You mean you used our cash to fund your weekend?'

'That's why he had us sleeping three in a bed'

'And Chalky and me in sleeping bags'

'Aye, and me out in the corridor'

'Shut up, you got a new suit out of it'

'And his wicked way with the landlady'

'You're a thievin' bastird,' growled Jock.

'Steady on now lads. It's only money,' soothed Ginger, 'how about a whip round?'

Printed in Great Britain
by Amazon.co.uk, Ltd.,
Marston Gate.